To order additional copies of this book, contact:
Xlibris Corporation
1-888-795-4274
www.Xlibris.com
Orders@Xlibris.com

# Creative Living Series:
# I Love My Parents
# and
# They Love Me!
## A children's book & parents' guidebook

By Catherine D. Weathers

Parents this Children's book is a basic beginner book that you can read to your child at an early age. This book is interactive and helps you assist your youngster prepare for preschool. It is simple to read and uses one of the best systems while reading it to your child. First read the story than allow your child to answer the questions the child in the story asked. Have your child repeat the alphabets and numbers. Let them name the colors and shapes. Make this time fun for both you and your child. It helps both parent and child express their feelings of love for each other. This book can be used as an alternative learning tool in preschool and kindergarten.

Hi, I am Josh

What is your name

I am a baby and my parents love me! I know they love me because they take good care of me. They feed me and dress me in fancy clothes. Although I do not like clothes they keep me warm.

I love my parents and they love me!

**Parents the Bible teach:** "Children are a gift from God,"

My Mom taught me how to pray in the morning, will you pray with me

Dear Lord, Thank you for a new day.

Bless my family, friends and people we meet today and bless the breakfast we eat. Amen!

I love my Mom and my Mommy loves me!

**Parents the Bible teaches:** "Train up a child in the way he should go: and when he is old he will not depart from it," Prov. 22:6.

# 1 year old I can help around the house.

At one year old I learned to walk and run. I play with my toys and make a mess.

Mom said, "Josh it time to put the toys away." I show my love by helping Mom clean-up my mess by learning how to put my toys away.

I love my Mom and my Mom loves me!

At two, Mom told me I am growing and I am a big boy! I can help pick up my things and put them away all by myself. Today Mom is taking me on a play date I am going to the park to meet my friend Ruth. Ruth's Dad does not live with her, yet he brings her to the park every Saturday to play while her Mommy is at work. I love Ruth and she loves me we are friends. I love my Mom and My Mom loves me!

At **2** year old I can do little task on my own.

Hi, Ruth!

Hi, Josh! Josh I am learning my alphabets.

What are alphabets, Ruth!

Ruth singing: a, b, c, d, e, f, g, h, I, j, k, l, m, n, o, p, q, r, s, t, u, v, w, x, y, z, now I know my a,b,c's can you say them with me.

I like that song, Ruth can you teach me. Yes, Josh just repeat after me, A,B,C,D.

At **2¹/²** year old I can begin to sing memory songs and write my name.

Ruth: my Mommy said I am a big girl now and I go to school. School is fun I am learning how to write my name. I play with other children my age.

Josh: my Mom said, "I am a big boy now, do you think I will be going to school soon"

Ruth: Maybe!

Well it is time to go I will see you later, Ruth.

Ruth has been toilet trained since 1 years old, she learned by watching her mom. She is ready for preschool and she enjoys it and shares her joy with her friend Josh.

Mom, Ruth goes to school she taught me a song A, B, C, D. Will I go to school

Yes, Josh you will go to school once you are potty trained. What is potty trained

You need to do your business in the toilet like all big boys and girls. But until you do I will help you learn the alphabet song and write your name, address and telephone number so you will be ready for school.

Okay! I love you Josh. Okay,

Mom, I love you!

I do not like to potty, but it makes Mom happy. I show my love by doing what my parents ask. While I am on the potty I am learning how to count.

I can count to ten, would you help me count to ten

1, 2, 3, 4, 5, 6, 7, 8, 9, 10 let's do it again
1, 2, 3, 4, 5, 6, 7, 8, 9, 10 now try saying it by yourself Josh!
Come on you can do it!
Great job!

I love my mom and my mom loves me!

**Parents,** repetition will help your child to memorize all letters, numbers shapes and word.

I know how to pray, count, sing the alphabet song and write my name and address I am almost ready for school.

I am learning how to say my telephone number. My Mom praise me every time I learn a new thing. She said I will be ready for school soon and when I go to school I will make lots of friends and behave myself. I love my Mom and my Mom shows me her love by teaching me!

Soughtout Family Day Care, Inc.

Children, obey your parents in the Lord: for this is right,
Eph. 6:1.

I must be polite and show my manners. I must say hi, to everyone when I enter a room. I must say thank you when people do good things for me. I must not beg for money or ask for another person's things. I must wait my turn and raise my hand when I need to go to the bathroom or when I need something while I am in school. I must ask the teacher's permission before leaving my seat. I must not hit or fight the other kids. When I am good my behavior shows my parents that I love them. I love my parents and they love me!

Dad said, if someone tries to hurt me I must tell the teacher than come home and tell Mom and Dad. If someone touch me in a manner I do not like I must tell Mom and Dad. I must listen in school and not talk while my teacher is talking. I am not to talk back to adults. When I am not sure about what to do I must ask the teacher for help. I love my Dad and my Daddy loves me, we have man to man talks that does not always feel nice, yet he has my best interest at heart. So I try my best to obey what my parents say! I love my parents and they love me!

At **3** years old I started school.

Now I am potty trained and today I start school. I am happy! My first day and we learned about colors and shapes. I meet a friend name Tom. I like School! I love Mom she brought me to school today.

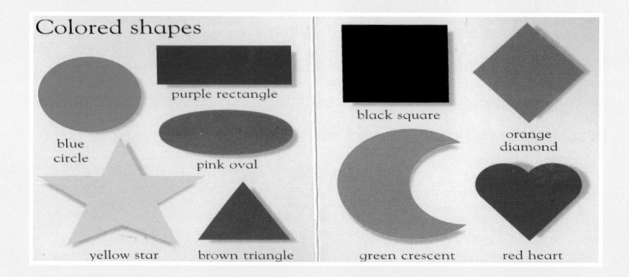

Colored shapes

blue circle

purple rectangle

pink oval

yellow star

brown triangle

black square

orange diamond

green crescent

red heart

At **4** years old I happily play with friends.

I played ring-a-round the rosy with my new friends and now it is time to leave.
Good-bye see you tomorrow! Dad picked me up from school. I love my Dad and he shows me he loves me, he picks me up from school.

This is the day the Lord has made; Let us rejoice and be glad today, Ps. 118:24.

Hi Mom, said Josh!

When I got home my Mom was cooking dinner. I sat at the tablet to complete my homework while Mom cooked she helped me with my homework by reading words I did not know. I love my Mom and My Mom loves me!

Mom: How was your day

Josh: Great Mom I made new friends and played lots of games. You were right I like school. I need to write my name and write my numbers for homework today.

Mom: Write nearly and do not erase.

Josh: Thank you, Mom for showing me how to write my name before I started school. Now I can do my homework by myself with little help, I am a big boy.

Mom: Josh you are really a big boy now, I am so proud of you, I love you.

I love you too Mom.

I love my parents and my parents love me!

My Dad always pray at the dinner table. Thank you, heavenly Father for the food we are about to eat .

Thank you for keeping my family safe, my job busy and for all my family and friends. Amen!

I love my Dad and he loves me, he shows me how to pray at supper and to take care of my things like he take care of Mommy and me.

I will praise you, Lord, with all my heart, Ps. 9:1.

After dinner I was able to watch my favorite T.V. show about animals before taking my bath and going to bed. Bath time is fun. I like to play with my duck.

I love my parents and they love me!

At **5** years old I can bathe with little assistance.

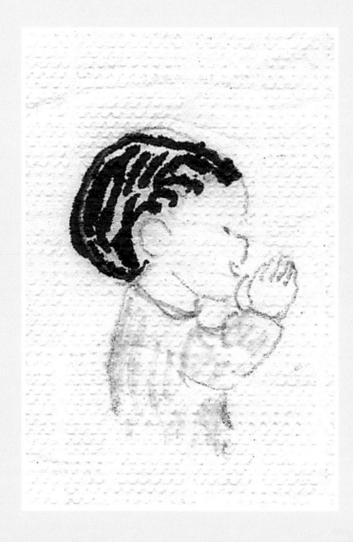

I pray every night before I go to sleep. Would you like to pray with me

Dear Lord,
Bless everyone, thank you for a good day, for keeping Mom and Dad safe. Thank you God, for my teacher and my new friends help us have fun. Thank you for all that you have given me and please keep me safe while I sleep, Amen. I love my parents and they love me!

# Good Night!

Printed in the United States
by Baker & Taylor Publisher Services